CHICO
and the
CHALLENGING TREE

by Peter Di Lisi
illustrated by Brant David

AuthorHouse™
1663 Liberty Drive
Bloomington, IN 47403
www.authorhouse.com
Phone: 1-800-839-8640

Published by AuthorHouse 10/02/2014

ISBN: 978-1-4969-4329-3 (sc)
ISBN: 978-1-4969-4332-3 (e)

Library of Congress Control Number: 2014917701

Print information available on the last page.

authorHOUSE®

CHICO
and the
CHALLENGING TREE

Our story begins with a bird in the sky.
He flew on down to see this furry little guy.

This furry guy was small but also very spunky.
His name was Chico, and he was the smallest little monkey.

The bird looked at the Chico and had something to say.

"I saw something amazing on the top of that tree, just the other day."

Chico the monkey was excited, he could tell it was something he would want to go see.

But the bird gave him a second look and said, "naaa you're too little to get up that tree!"

Chico the monkey was shocked, as he watched the bird smile and then fly away.

"It doesn't matter what that bird thinks," Chico said "I will climb to the top, even if it takes me all day."

As Chico looked up, he wished
like the bird he could fly too.

But since Chico couldn't he
started to climb, because
that's what monkeys do.

8

The first few branches were easy, but Chico still had a long way to go.

The higher he went and further he got, Chico started going a little too slow.

"Maybe the bird was right," he said "and this tree is just too tall.

Maybe I will never reach to the top, maybe I shouldn't even try at all."

All of a sudden through the whistling winds a little voice saying "you can do it" he could hear.

It came from a tiny caterpillar, and the message he had was very clear.

The caterpillar said "What does size have to do with where you want to go? The only way you will find out if you can do it, is to give it a shot and then will you know."

Now even though the caterpillar was tiny, Chico must have thought he had a big brain in his head.

Because instead of giving up and going back down, Chico decided to keep going instead.

The caterpillar said "good luck my friend, I will see you at the end of the day.

I will meet you on the top of this tree after my nap, is it a deal, what do you say?"

Chico nodded his head with a big smile, and said "I will do my best not to stop!"

Even though he had no idea how this tiny caterpillar would make his own way to the top.

Chico had his goals very high, and from where he stood seemed very hard to reach.

He knew it would be tough getting there and definitely no day at the beach.

A slithering snake hissed at Chico, for his efforts to make it to the top.

"You might as well just give up now" He said,
"There is no shame in wanting to stop".

But Chico really wanted to make it and said
"I am going to continue anyway.

It doesn't matter what that snake thinks " Chico said
"I will climb to the top, even if it takes me all day".

As Chico passed the next few branches,
a chimpanzee passed by him with also
something to say.

"You're crazy if you think you're getting to
the top "he said, "I am so much bigger and
only made it halfway".

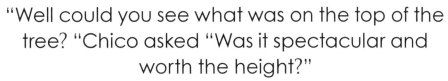

"Well could you see what was on the top of the tree? "Chico asked "Was it spectacular and worth the height?"

"Nope," said the chimp "it was too hard to see, and it was still way out of sight."

"If you are smart like me, you will head back down and not waste your time."

"You don't even know what's up that tree, it might not be worth the climb."

Chico said "Well that is just you, you're not me, and it's too bad you couldn't make it all the way"

It doesn't matter what that chimp thinks "Chico said "I will climb to the top, even if it takes me all day."

The closer Chico got, the harder it was to reach the branches up above.

As another animal shared his thoughts, it was a grumpy morning dove.

"It's getting pretty late don't you think?"
he said "You're moving as fast as a slug.

I can't believe you're actually giving this
a shot... You're really going to listen to
that bug?"

22

Chico looked at the dove and said "The caterpillar just pointed out what I have been thinking all along."

"It doesn't matter about my size you see , as long as my will stays nice and strong.

I am going to keep moving no matter how slow I go, so if you don't mind please move out of the way.

It doesn't matter what that dove thinks," Chico said "I will climb to the top, even if it takes me all day."

So through the wind and the rain,
Chico kept on going, he gave it everything that he had.

He finally made it up to the top, because he didn't give up
and that made him feel very glad.

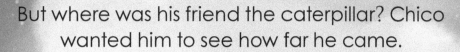

But where was his friend the caterpillar? Chico
wanted him to see how far he came.

If not for his words of wisdom, Chico's ending would
have not been the same.

Chico was about to head down to get his new friend,
and bring him up So the victory they could share.

But little did he know, there was no need to go down,
for the caterpillar was already there.

You see, while the caterpillar was napping a transformation had begun.

Before he took his nap a great cocoon he had spun.

Just like Chico, he had a goal to achieve.

And to make it all happen all he needed was to believe.

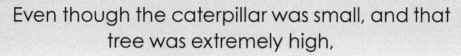

Even though the caterpillar was small, and that
tree was extremely high,

He did not let that stop him for a second, from
turning into a butterfly.

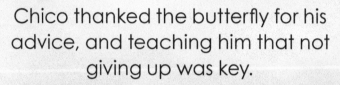

Chico thanked the butterfly for his advice, and teaching him that not giving up was key.

They sat together and enjoyed the sight, it was the biggest banana Chico ever did see.

"Push yourself to the limits,
leave all your fears behind,

And in the end if you don't give up,
you just might be surprised what you will find".

By Peter Di Lisi

CPSIA information can be obtained
at www.ICGtesting.com
Printed in the USA
LVHW07s2240220818
587687LV00004B/6/P

When Chico the monkey
becomes curious to see
what's at the top of a great
tall tree, he gives it all he can
to reach his goal.

In his journey, he faces many
challenges and learns that
will power and determination
can take even the smallest
monkey to the most
unimaginable places.

authorHOUSE®

ISBN 978-1-4969-4329-

5149

9 781496 943293

CHICO
and the
VERY BAD and NO GOOD DAY

by Peter Di Lisi

illustrated by Brant David

To Elena

When it rains always
look up...that way
you will always see
the rainbows.

Peter D